Movies Made In Ireland

Ryan's Daughter

By Aubrey Dillon Malone

GLI Limited
The Tower Enterprise Centre
Pearse Street
Dublin 2, Ireland
Tel: +353 1 6775655
Fax: +353 1 6775487
E-Mail: towerctr@iol.ie

First published by GLI Limited, 1996
© GLI Limited

© Text Copyright A. Dillon-Malone
Editor: Pat Neville
Typesetting & Layout: Alan Smyth Studios

ISBN: 1 900480 20 4

ACKNOWLEDGMENTS
Turner Entertainment Co.
Peter Vollebregt
Joe Reynolds

All photographs © Turner Entertainment Co.

All rights reserved. No part of this publication may be reproduced or transmitted in any form or by any means, electronic or mechanical, including photocopy, recording or any information storage and retrieval system without the permission of the publishers in writing.

CONTENTS

INTRODUCTION - 10

THE CAST - 18

PROBLEMS ON THE SET - 32

CRITICAL RECEPTION - 46

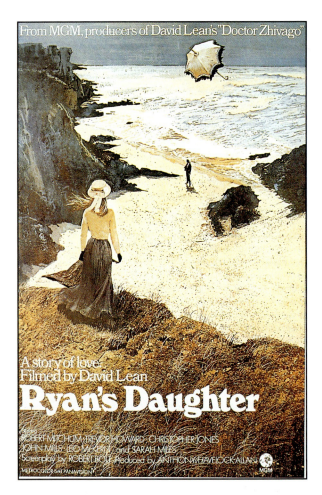

Ryan's Daughter

Starring:
Robert Mitchum
Sarah Miles
Trevor Howard
Christopher Jones
John Mills
Leo McKern
Barry Foster

Director:
David Lean

Year: 1970

INTRODUCTION

The year was 1969. There was a director who was tired of making epics and wanted a human story. An actor tired of playing beefcakes. And an actress who had a guilt complex because her husband wrote the script...

Little did David Lean know what awaited him when he took on the task of making *Ryan's Daughter*. He envisaged the film as a vignette, but twelve months and many millions of dollars later, it was more akin to a Frankenstein. This was due not only to the erratic meteorological conditions of West Kerry, but also on-the-set friction, freak accidents, and a constantly changing narrative perspective. When the film finally wrapped, having made many of the locals at least temporarily rich and many others permanently restless - having tasted their seven minutes of fame they found it difficult to regress to their quote unquote Ordinary Lives - Lean and his cast and crew were totally exhausted.

When Robert Bolt sent Lean the script, his first reaction was 'no' - just as Robert Mitchum's would be. Often in the months to come, he would wonder if that first reaction mightn't have been the wiser one.

Bolt wrote it for his then wife Sarah Miles, an instinctive, evocative actress who hadn't elevated herself to the A-League as yet. Would *Ryan's Daughter* be the vehicle to effect this transition?

Lean originally tinkered with the idea of setting it in India. He settled on Ireland finally because he needed a political superstructure to amplify the romantic theme and flesh it out. As things worked out, many people felt mixing his drinks like this was a foolish move which compromised both elements.

Based loosely on the story of *Madame Bovary* - though few critics picked up on the connection - the film chronicled the fate of diffident schoolteacher Charles Shaughnessy (Robert Mitchum) who's cuckolded by his flirtatious wife Rosy Ryan (Sarah Miles) after shellshocked World War One veteran Randolph Doryan (Christopher Jones) arrives in Ireland. Doryan has been assigned to Ireland to suppress operations between the IRA and German spies, the film being set in 1916 at the height of the war.

It was a simple story, too simple perhaps for some, but it crystallised much of what was endemic in Irish life - the struggle against The Auld Enemy, forbidden love, parochial prudery, infidelity, idealism, betrayal, shattered dreams and a cautious optimism about the future. Lean set it on the grand scale, as was his wont, but he also captured the frustration of smalltown lives with all their parish pump begrudgery. This was a *Valley of the Squinting*

Windows for the seventies, an (O) Irish parable of lust and retribution, and Mitchum's stolid fortitude was perfectly set off by Miles' erotic yearning and Jones' twitchy confusion.

The Dingle peninsula was the venue. Here, 200 Irish workers undertook the work of building 40 full-scale structures, using over 800 tons of rough-hewn granite. There would be shops, houses, a school, a church and - inevitably - a pub. The village was christened Kirrary.

Dingle never had it so good. The natives rented their cottages and moved into caravans themselves. Hollywood had just been a word for these people heretofore; now, suddenly, it had come to Dunquin, Kerry's last resort - literally. On a clear day, the locals joked, you could see the Statue of Liberty.

A fictional village was constructed for the film, a kind of forerunner of *Glenroe* on a larger scale, with sepia-tinged postcards of

Director David Lean overlooks the construction of the fictional village of Kirrary.

it being sold to all and sundry as it became as real as any of the actual villages around.

The area throbbed with activity as hundreds of erstwhile out-of-work fishermen suddenly found themselves in lucrative jobs. The pubs too - there was one for each week of the year, according to Miles - were filled to capacity. It must have been as much a culture shock for the natives as it was for the wide-eyed visitors, who may only have heard of the Irish penchant for the *'craic'* at second hand.

With the exception of one Robert Mitchum.

So lively were Mitchum's parties in the hotel he all but took over for the shoot, one wag said the studio should dump the movie and release the parties...

THE CAST

Mitchum was taken by the script on his first reading, claiming it was the best thing he had been presented with in years. He had just finished a rash of eminently forgettable westerns like *The Good Guys and the Bad Guys*, *Young Billy Young*, *Villa Rides* and *Five Card Stud*, and was thoroughly disenchanted with the movie business and his own increasingly empty place in it. *Ryan's Daughter* looked like just the ticket to end all that, but leafing through the script he noticed that his own character was in practically every scene. *Ergo*, less time off.

He was also wary of the protracted shooting schedule. 'I didn't figure I could keep myself glued together long enough,' was how he put it. When Lean offered him the part, he said he was definitely interested, but had planned to commit suicide and the role would scupper such a

Robert Mitchum who plays the local school-teacher Charles Shaughnessy.

resolve. This was a vintage Mitchum oneliner but Lean was up to it. 'Well if you will just do this wretched little film of ours,' he replied, 'I'll be happy to stand the expenses of your funeral.'

He agreed to do it upon such a whimsical note, but not before he had organised official mini-holidays in the middle of the shoot.

Miles was uncomfortable in the part of Rosy, feeling that some would say she landed it because she was married to Bolt. She wanted to do a screen test to allay such rumours, but Lean refused. She was roughly the same age as Mills' two daughters Hayley and Juliet, and felt he wanted one of them to get the part. Far from acting the prima donna, she approached the set each day with a growing trepidation. Being the wife of the screenwriter, she said, was 'a gruesome disadvantage, because every day I'd have to prove myself *doubly* able.'

Lean was captivated by Mitchum's ability

Sarah Miles as Rosy.

to laugh and joke with the crew between takes (how else could he keep his sanity over the ten months, he mused) and then step into character almost instantaneously when the cameras rolled. When asked what his secret was, he said he wasn't sure, that he didn't think too much about it. 'Do you go to school to be tall?' he asked, rhetorically. 'Do you go to school to be blonde? Talent is like having an ear for pitch. You can't develop it.'

Mitchum enjoyed himself immensely baiting Lean, pitting his laidback American personality against the Englishman's more refined, cerebral brain. He threw hippie slang at him, and embarrassed him hugely with irreverent ripostes during the shooting of the sensitive wedding night scene with Rosy.

'The difference between us,' Mitchum chuckled one day, 'is that he speaks English and I speak American.'

Mitchum didn't only raise hell on the set, but also after hours in his hotel suite,

which became a kind of Mecca for any fun-lover within a twenty mile radius. It was a far cry from the character of the repressed Charles Shaughnessy, but Mitchum, consummate pro that he was, negotiated the transition each morning as he donned the crumpled garb of the dour schoolteacher.

'I just show up and do it,' he often commented when he was asked what his secret was. A complicated man who acted simply, he flattered to deceive and worked hard to make it look easy. In a sense he pre-dated the 'don't just do something, stand there' style of (non) acting customised by the likes of Clint Eastwood and Charles Bronson in later times. Anybody who ever acted with him, however, and that included Sarah Miles, was captivated by his animal magnetism and craggy vulnerability. Nobody has ever been able to quite define what 'star quality' is, but Mitchum had it to spare.

Trevor Howard was given the part of

Father Collins. It wasn't exactly a taxing role - the priest saw everything in black and white, no more than the Captain Bligh of *Mutiny on the Bounty* - but sometimes these are the most difficult to play. It was essentially a thankless role but Howard, consummate character actor that he was, gave it 110%.

No less a luminary than Marlon Brando had been inked in for the role of Major Doryan originally, but he cried off after under-going difficulties with his film *Quiemada* in the Caribbean. Richard Burton and Peter O'Toole had also been considered, but Lean eventually decided on relative unknown Christopher Jones to play the part. It wasn't a decision he would regret, but Jones gave him his fair share of headaches on the set.

Jones had had a troubled past. As was the case with James Dean, an actor he would often be compared with, his mother had died young and he became unfocussed and rebellious as a result. Dean's epochal movie *Rebel Without a Cause* had a huge effect on him, virtually copperfastening his decision to make a career in films, and it seemed to be just another part of the jigsaw when he married Susan Strasberg, the daughter of Method guru Lee. The ink was hardly dry on the wedding certificate before they parted, and the Christopher Jones who took on the part of Doryan was almost as emotionally turbulent as that man himself. Lean would liked to have milked that turbulence for dramatic effect, but Jones - like Dean - was an uncommunicative soul and turned his talent on and off like a tap. A bit like the Irish weather, actually. No wonder Lean was having headaches....

Jones was a minimalist actor, somebody who understood the camera well and operated on the nuance, the half-caught glance. He was always going to be diametrically opposed to Lean, who treated his actors like an anglicised Hitchcock, having his blueprint drawn up before he shouted 'Action'. In the scene

Christopher Jones who plays
the British Army major Randolph Doryan.

where Doryan first meets Rosy, Jones underplayed his shellshock and Lean was seriously unimpressed. It was only when he saw the rushes he realised what Jones was at.

The love scene between Rosy and Doryan in the woods was another bugbear for Lean. Sarah Miles had made no secret of her feelings of annoyance towards Jones on the set, and when it came time to do this pivotal scene - where Rosy finally gives vent to the passion denied her in Shaughnessy's marital bed - Jones kept postponing doing it, telling Lean she didn't attract him physically. This should have been irrelevant anyway for a professional actor, but Jones' motives were personal. Miles was distraught as a result, as was Lean, who would even have considered sacking Jones if he hadn't already shot so much footage of him.

Lean received his most pleasant acting surprise in John Mills, who went against the grain of decades of stiff upper lip military types to throw himself full tilt into the role of Michael, the mute, physically-challenged village idiot.

Mills was delighted with the simplicity of his make-up: twisted mouth, shaved eyebrows, gap-toothed smile, false nose, streels of hair hanging from a bald pate. Add a querulous expression and a deranged walk and you had a character whose mannerisms almost did his acting for him.

Mills actually went on to win an Oscar for the part - repeating the achievement of Jane Wyman, who was also honoured thusly for essaying a role in which she didn't even have one line of dialogue in 1948. Mills was understandably chuffed, and commented proudly from the platform of the Dorothy Chandler Pavilion on the night of his presentation: 'Winning the Oscar signifies many things, not least among them the fact that I no longer have to be known in Hollywood as Hayley Mills' father.'

PROBLEMS ON THE SET

Lean's practice of shooting infinitely more footage than he needed, while laudatory from an artistic point of view, had its downside for certain actors. Niall Toibin, to name but one of these, had quite a sizeable role in the first cut, which ran to a whopping 11½ hours, but when Lean whittled it all down to 3½ hours, Toibin was virtually excised from the film.

The cast signed on for a six-month stint but it ended up as exactly double that. Mitchum, an impatient man at the best of times, was most affected by the delays. Lean was also infuriated, even if many of them were of his own making. The combination of his punctiliousness and the fact that it was difficult to shoot more than a couple of minutes of footage at a time - neither thr sun nor the dull weather

Sarah Miles and David Lean discuss the next scene.

stayed sunny or dull long enough to get a full day's work in - meant that tempers were almost continually frayed. Mitchum did his best to lighten the atmosphere, but it wasn't always possible. The film was enough to cure anyone of location shooting.

Making the movie totally on location was a courageous decision. It meant infinitely more control for Lean (an avowed control freak) but aso infinitely more headaches. The weather was the obvious minus. The cast sat out many hours waiting for the sun to turn to rain, or the rain to sun, equally frustrated about the fact that the only thing you could say for sure about the Irish weather was that there was no one one thing you could say for sure about the Irish weather. When George Stevens was shooting *Shane* in 1952, he had waited months for a certain cloud formation in Jackson Hole, Wyoming. David Lean was similar in the sense that he wanted the

Charles and Rosy leave behind their childhood village to embark on an uncertain future.

elements to act as an objective correlative of the emotional action.

Mitchum became infuriated by the incessant stoppages and delays, claiming he was even too bored to drink. He conducted an interview with a member of the press one day from a position of lying down in his trailer with a wide-brimmed hat over his face. The journalist wrote in his article that it was the first time he had ever interviewed anyone who was talking through his hat. Mitchum was incensed , as well he might have been. He was also incensed by Lean's perfectionism. 'He shoots the film,' he said, 'then he re-shoots it. Then he looks at it all and shoots it again.' This was not, repeat not, the philosophy of the man who survived because he worked cheap and didn't take up too much time. Lean he might have been, but he certainly wasn't 'lean'.

Mitchum also had trouble trying to resemble a schoolteacher rather than a hunk who had just walked off the lot of a

cowboy film by mistake. 'No matter what they do,' he quipped, 'from the back I'm going to look like a Bulgarian wrestler.' Three months and a million dollars later, however, the gentle giant was comfortable with his wardrobe, Trevor Howard having been padded up to look normal by comparison.

A number of freakish accidents on the beleaguered movie set also caused undue delays. Jones smashed up his Ferrari one day in a burst of James Dean style eccentricity, and two Land Rovers got stuck in a peat bog in another instance. Both John Mills and Trevor Howard were also almost drowned when their boat capsized one day. It hit Mills on the head and knocked him out. He was drifting out to sea when he was rescued by two frogmen and brought to hospital.

Mills showed a lot of foresight by taking out the false set of teeth which make-up artist Charlie Parker had given him, fearing that if the boat did capsize, he might

Trevor Howard as the local priest Father Collins.

swallow them. When someone rushed up to Parker after the incident and asked him if he had heard Mills nearly drowned, he growled, 'Never mind about Johnny. Where are my f***ing teeth!' Christianity indeed.

Apart from the weather and the dangers of filming, Lean's main problem was Jones, whose behaviour became increasingly more difficult as time went on. Mooning about the place like Marlon Brando crossed with Montgomery Clift, he was either totally immersed in his character or intimidated by Miles. Also, he was shattered to hear about the murder of Sharon Tate, news of which came through as the film was being shot. He had had a romance with Tate in Rome shortly before Lean offered him this role, and lived in fear that Roman Polanski would seek revenge if he was ever allowed back on American soil.

Jones also refused to put on a British accent for the part, and refused to work on

Sundays due to religious principles. Lean tried to keep his temper under control, as did Miles and the other crew members. The budget was soaring out of all control and they were way behind schedule.

The experience wasn't exactly what Miles anticipated, and after the film was finished - finally - she emoted, 'Filming is a frustrating, unfulfilling process only made bearable by those few minutes a day, five maybe, of genuine creativity between 'Action' and 'Cut'.'

Everybody was exhausted when the last take was put in the can. The experience, said Mitchum, was 'like building the Taj Mahal with matchsticks.' David Lean, who had perhaps made one big budget movie too many, would know the feeling.

Rosy and Doryan spend time together against the backdrop of the beautiful Dingle peninsula.

CRITICAL RECEPTION

The press were harsh on the movie, *The Sun* calling it 'an all-star, six million quid bore' and *The Times* saying it was 'too bad even to be funny'. People voted with their feet, however. It ran for nearly a year in a central Dublin cinema, which had to prove some kind of a point about what the public wanted and what po-faced critics felt they *ought* to want.

Lean had been accused of being 'pretty' in *Dr Zhivago* and in *Ryan's Daughter* many believed he was taking up where he left off in the earlier movie, re-visiting old terrain, grafting large emotions onto ordinary people against the backdrop of the elements in order to give the illusion of profundity.

Most of the critics seemed to be in

John Mills as the mute village idiot Michael.

consensus about the overall inadvisability of the project. The acerbic Pauline Kael said it was 'gush made respectable by millions of dollars tastefully wasted'. Alexander Walker opined, 'Instead of looking like the money it cost to make, it feels like the time it took to shoot.'

Angela Allen claimed it was a grandiose yarn that worked adequately on the level of an old fashioned woman's magazine story, but any greater pretensions were ruined by Lean's overblown direction. Leonard Maltin felt that the breathtaking scenery dwarfed Robert Bolt's thin storyline.

Luke Gibbons said the film provided 'a much-needed break from the escapism and mythology which has vitiated so much Irish cinema.' But as he also went on to point out, it was hardly the vanguard of realism either. The women did little but gossip in it, while the men either spent their time hurling, boozing or maligning Rosy Ryan. None of them seemed to have jobs, nor to be particularly concerned about that fact. (The manner in which they eventually converge upon 'the major's whore' and exact tribal revenge upon her, in fact, is like something out of a primeval melodrama.)

Though the film was set in Ireland, this was only an incidental matter to Lean. He felt his story had a universal appeal. Posterity would appear to have proved him right. Robert Bolt said he was looking for 'emotional size' rather than stage-Irish whimsy. Many, however, felt that the latter element guillotined the former - and that the impact created by the rugged emotions and equally rugged landscape was neutralised by hackneyed attitudes to passionate Irish maidens and decent, clumsy menfolk. Neither did the presence of the loutish villagers - who seemed to both think and act with one central mind - help. Nor the fact that the love scene between Rosy and Doryan in the woods looked more like a sumptuous ad by

B*ord Fáilte* than the acting out of a long-dormant passion, what with its lingering shots, its gossamer, its flowers and its wild, wild winds.

The film was nominated for four Oscars but only Freddy Young (for his wonderful cinematography) and John Mills, who, like Mitchum, stepped out of character to play the village idiot, got the nod. It was a vindication of sorts for Lean, who had nursed his project through all the bad times and even spent two years in pre-production with it. If the critics were unimpressed, well maybe they always had been.

As Sarah Miles put it, 'When *Lawrence of Arabia* came out, they called it 'The Four Pillars of Boredom'. Then *Dr Zhivago* came out and they said 'Oh what a shame - it isn't as good as *Lawrence of Arabia*; David Lean has lost his touch'. Then he does *Ryan's Daughter* and they say, 'Not a patch on *Dr Zhivago*'. There might be a lesson there for all budding directors who

page 51

imagine they're going to get a fair shake from those who use pens like scalpels.

A lot of the negative feeling about the film came from bitterness among people in the industry about the fact that Lean was being given such large budgets at a time when studios were cutting their cloth to the measure. Experimental film-makers, they argued, could make a half dozen features with the kind of money Lean was being vouchsafed for one. This was hardly the point, however. Lean was a proven talent with a track record of classics and semi-classics behind him, and he had to be given his head. The bottom line is that *Ryan's Daughter* has grown with time. Posterity has been kind to it, unlike the critics of its day. How many shoestring-budgeted features of the same time are still remembered in the nineties?

Lean almost felt afraid to go out on the street as a result of all the spleen vented on the film by its many detractors. Pauline Kael was the most vocal culprit, but other critics queued up to lionise it as well. It was so long in the works, too much was expected of it. Many people claimed that it was just another empty box of chocolates from a director noted for making bland epics that looked too doctored to convince.

Nigel Andrews wrote: 'the plethora of eyecatching backcloths not only dwarfs the characters - as it did in *Zhivago* and *Lawrence* - but dilutes the pastoral-tragic idiom to produce a mere escapist dream, the tragedy and moral conflict alike dissolving in the aesthetic explosion of the scenery.' Translated into English, one may take this to mean Andrews feels the film looks better than it sounds.

The endless duration, it was also noted, amplified the script's weaknesses rather than camouflaging them. In this sense, Lean's penchant for the big sweep almost proved his undoing. In a sense, it was a film both praised and blamed for the wrong things. John Mills earned most of

the kudos, but the fact remains that his was a much overwrought performance.

In severe need of a visit to the dentist, Michael looked for all the world like Dingle's answer to the Hunchback of Notre Dame, a grotesque but gentle commentor on the action. It was a one-dimensional turn, but that one dimension was still impressive enough to win him the ultimate accolade. Once again, the Academy showed its favouritism to a nominee with a disability. The truth of the matter is that it's much more difficult to give a memorable performance with a normal nose, two ears and one's own full set of teeth. Mills, however, garnered enough pathos to win the sentimental vote.

What most people rightly agreed on was the manner in which Robert Mitchum acquitted himself so admirably. The character of Shaughnessy was almost like a repudiation of everything he had done before, but he underplayed it to perfection. Derek Malcolm wrote of him: 'Had it not been for his presence - and the word is apposite - I do not believe there would have been a film at all. Everyone else acts like Trojans, but Mitchum is simply and gloriously himself. Even when he's off the screen he casts his shadow. It only makes everyone else, not least David Lean, look small.'

Lean himself echoed that view when he said, 'After twenty years of playing a comic strip character called Superstud, Mitchum at last is being recognised as the gifted actor he has always been. He is a master of stillness. Other actors act; Mitchum is. He has true delicacy and expressiveness, but his *forte* is indelible identity. Simply by being there, he can make almost any other actor look like a hole on the screen.'

From another point of view, maybe that was the main problem with the film. The last thing any director wants in an epic is the ordinary guy stealing the show.

Whatever acrimony we may heap on it, however, it remains, as Mitchum put it, 'Lean's love affair with Ireland'.

The film wins out by playing its hand close to its chest. Lean doesn't commit himself as to where his affiliations lie. Neither does he condemn. We don't dislike anyone except Tom Ryan, the traitor. Everyone else is just a victim of circumstance...or their own characters. Charles of his inhibition, Rosy of her shopsoiled dreams, Doryan because he simply happens to be in the the wrong place at the wrong time.

It's easy to criticise it for its air of pervading gloom, or the fact that it's discernably low on laughs, or the fact that the cast rarely threaten to become much more than contrived figures on Lean's lush landscape. We can even accuse it of buying into stereotyped concepts of village life, and an Ireland that has long been with O'Leary in the grave. But notwithstanding all this, it's beautiful to watch, it has a perennial message, and it achieves a kind of epiphany in the quiet dignity of the epilogue.

Rosy has to suffer for her sin of infidelity, as has Charles for his inability to satisfy her, and Doryan for committing the unpardonable sin of falling in love with another man's wife. All three members of the eternal triangle lose in this sense - but two of them seem intent on crawling from the psychic wreckage by the final frame.

Or maybe not...